Sammy Can't Swim

Written and Illustrated by Sue Thorman

Archway Publishing books may be ordered through booksellers or by contacting:

Archway Publishing
1663 Liberty Drive
Bloomington, IN 47403
www.archwaypublishing.com
844-669-3957

ISBN: 978-1-6657-2155-4 (sc)
ISBN: 978-1-6657-2154-7 (e)

Print information available on the last page.

Archway Publishing rev. date: 04/04/2022

Dedication

This book is dedicated to my late husband, Thomas. Although he left us way too early, his imprint on life and the people he touched was significant. He was always optimistic and full of life. He left a wealth of love for all that knew him. He was my heart and soul. I'm sure his heavenly vibrations are felt by many. If for a moment, we could fill our hearts with love, peace, and understanding.

Sometimes, it's not easy being me. I wish I had fins that worked, so I could swim with my friends.

These are my two
best friends.
Hi! Hi! Can you
help me?

I've always felt sad that I can't keep up like my friends. My fins are not as strong for some reason. They don't work.

So, I was thinking of my friends again. Hi guys!!! Where are you swimming today?

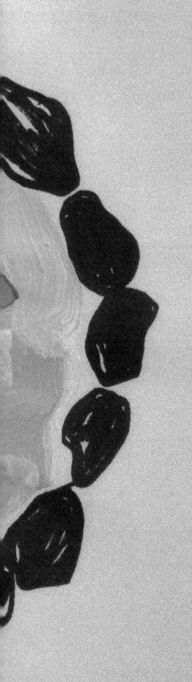

These are my girlfriends –
Susie & Sally.
They seem to understand
what I need.

I reached out to Charlie the crab. Charlie, Charlie... I need your help, but he was very crabby.

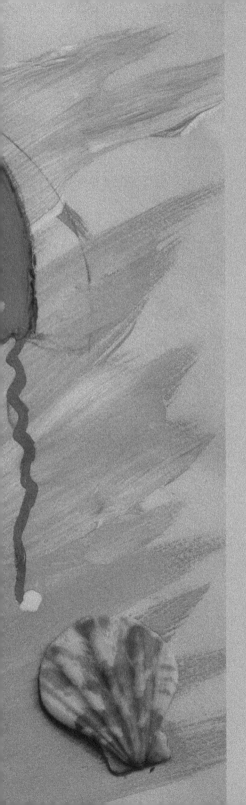

This is Johnny the jellyfish.
Hi Johnny!!! I was wondering
if you could push my fins
to start them up.

Help me please!
Just help me!!!

Of course, they all said!!!
Just watch us!!! Then,
do what we do!

19

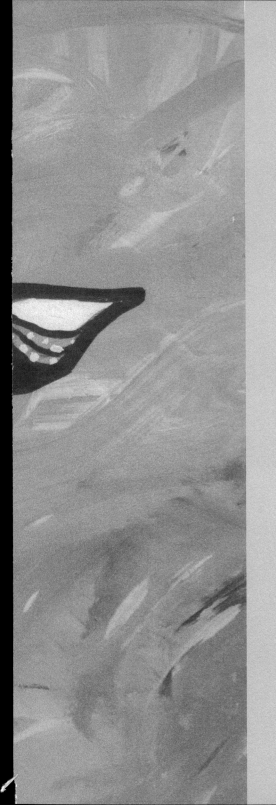

Wally the whale also wanted to help me. I am so lucky to have such good friends! Thanks Wally!!!

Yay!!! It's working!
It's working!
I can finally swim.
Thanks friends!!!

CPSIA information can be obtained
at www.ICGtesting.com
Printed in the USA
LVHW072024220723
753168LV00058B/1050